MW00928684

This notebook belongs to :

Made in the USA
Monee, IL
14 December 2021

85559880R00073